Matteo's New Hat

BY
Niki D'Alonzo Martinez

MATTEO'S NEW HAT

Illustrated By Kronosmond

ISBN: 9798862732290

Imprint: Independently published

For Matthew

Matteo was a little baby.
He loved to play with his toys.

Matteo especially
loved to sleep on his back.

Day after day his head
began to change shape.

Matteo visited a clinic.
He got to sit in a chair that
spins around and look at
twinkling lights.

So, Matteo got
a special new hat!

It even had dinosaurs on it
in all different colors.

At first, his hat felt
uncomfortable and different.

But as he wore it each day,
he got used to it.

He played, ate,
and even slept
with his hat on.

Sometimes when Matteo was at the park or taking a walk, people would stare or ask questions.

"What is that on his head?"
Or "Is he hurt?"

But his sister would say, "That's Matteo's special hat. Don't worry, he's OK!"

Matteo made sure to clean his special hat each day and to also take it off for a short break. Some days, he would want the hat back on right away.

Eventually his head changed shape because of the help from his special hat.

So, he said goodbye to his hat. He put it in a spot in his room where he can always find it when he wants to give it a big hug.

MATTEO'S NEW HAT

Made in the USA
Middletown, DE
23 April 2024